Gli anni di Nettuno sulla terra

Translated from Italian

The New Job & The Owl
Anna Ruchat

Translated from Italian by
Eleanor Chapman and Lucy Rand

First published in English by Strangers Press, Norwich, 2022
part of UEA Publishing Project

First published in Switzerland by Ibis Edizioni as
Gli anni di Nettuno sulla terra in 2018

All rights reserved
Author © Anna Ruchat, 2018
Translator © Eleanor Chapman and Lucy Rand, 2022

Printed by
Swallowtail, Norwich

Series editors
Nathan Hamilton & Lucy Rand

Editorial assistance
Lily Alden, Erin Maniatopoulou and Emma Seager

Proofread by
Senica Maltese

Cover design and typesetting
Glen Robinson (aka GRRR.UK)

Design Copyright © Glen Robinson, 2022

The rights of Anna Ruchat to be identified as the author
and Eleanor Chapman and Lucy Rand to be identified as the
translators of this work have been asserted in accordance with
the Copyright, Designs and Patents Act, 1988. This booklet is
sold subject to the condition that it shall not, by way of trade or
otherwise, be lent, resold, hired out, stored in a retrieval system,
or otherwise circulated without the publisher's prior consent
in any form of binding or cover other than that in which it is
published and without a similar condition including this condition
being imposed on the subsequent purchaser.

ISBN: 978-1-913861-43-8

The New Job and The Owl

Anna Ruchat

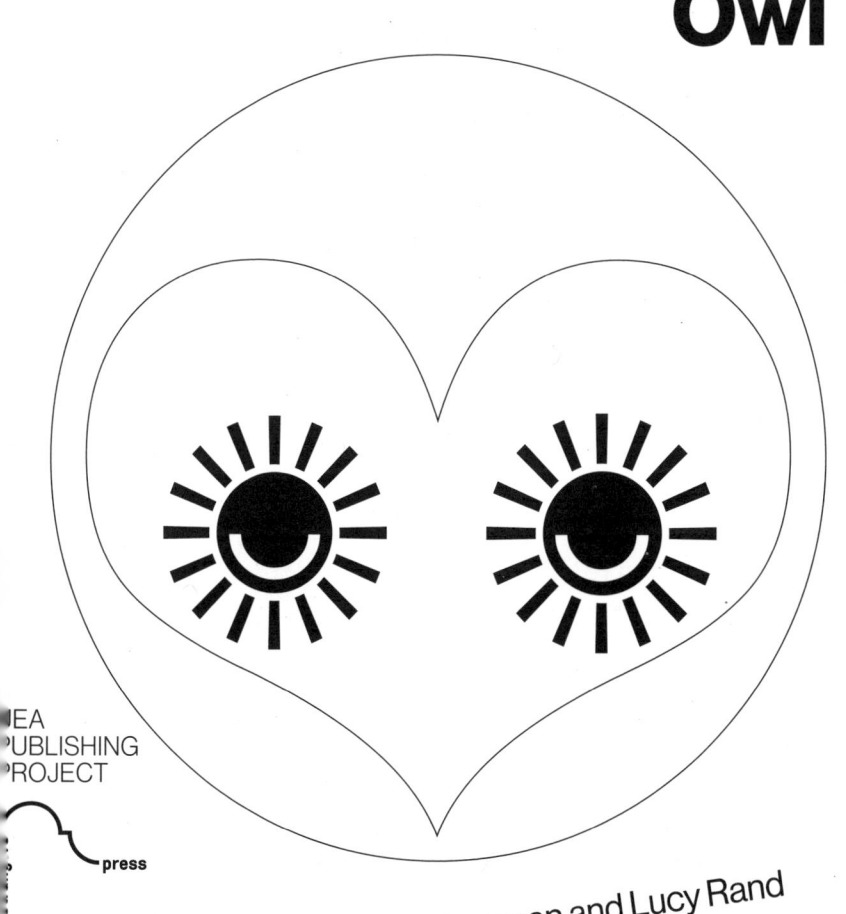

EA
PUBLISHING
PROJECT

press

Translated by Eleanor Chapman and Lucy Rand

'The thought flashed through Sonia's mind, wasn't he mad?
But she dismissed it at once:
No, it was something else.
She could make nothing of it, nothing!'

FYODOR DOSTOEVSKY
Crime and Punishment

17 JUNE 1983

Talk-show host Enzo Tortora is arrested by the Carabinieri di Roma under the orders of the Naples public prosecutor's office, charged with association with the Camorra.

THE NEW JOB

ONE LATE-JUNE DAY IN THE EARLY 1980s, a young girl from a poor and rather uncultured family was summoned for a job interview in a city in the German-speaking part of Switzerland. Teresa had been wanting to leave the valley of her birth for some time, but not to come back at the end of each day, like her father and brother did, on a bus teeming with cross-border workers. She wanted to leave in earnest, for another town or city, to meet new people, earn a small amount for herself each month and perhaps, later on, be able to send something home. These were just dreams.

    She was eighteen with a shy, oval face and dark eyes, thick eyebrows and jet black hair; you could tell just by looking at her that she was a bright girl and her father was very proud. He was the one who had suggested that she put an ad in the paper to be an au-pair. She was good with children, having practically raised her younger brothers, and she had a wonderful imagination. Although her limbs still lumbered with adolescent gracelessness, there were already in her the makings of a young woman.

Her father was a man of few words, short, wiry, his skin all cracked from the sun. He had hardly finished primary school and had been working as a bricklayer for over thirty years. Now, knowing neither how to write his daughter's advert nor which paper to send it to, he felt ashamed.

Still troubled by the unsettled matter of the advert, one day while mixing lime on site he saw the architect walking towards him over the concrete foundation of an unlaid floor and took him to one side to talk about his daughter and her desire to go away. Happy to help this bricklayer, who had struck him from the outset as one of the fastest and most thorough workers on site, the architect told him he would speak to his wife that evening and get back to him the following day. He was true to his word and turned up the next morning with an address and a telephone number. They were a family with two young children, the architect told him, friends of friends. Italians who had been living up north for a few years. The wife taught at the university — what exactly the bricklayer wasn't sure — and was out for most of the day. The husband was a doctor, he worked at a hospital (only in the mornings) and had a practice in the apartment next door to their very large home. They also had a woman come in for the cleaning, the architect added as if to reassure him, so the girl would only have the children to take care of: dropping them off and picking them up from nursery, spending a few hours in the park with them, giving them an afternoon snack and making their dinner. Basically, his impression, he said, a little embarrassed at having got carried away in the details, was that they were a decent family, and his daughter would be in good hands.

And so it was that Teresa left one morning in June. She got on the bus across the border which, as it was a Sunday, was half empty, and then caught the train to the city where she was expected for the interview. She wore a pair of dark trousers that her sister had bought for a relative's wedding, smart shoes and a flowery blouse from the year before that was now a little stretched over her bust. Her black hair was pulled back tightly into a thick, shoulder-length plait. She carried a patent leather handbag that her mother had insisted she borrow, inside which were her documents, train ticket and a book she had been given for her birthday by an older cousin. The woman she had spoken to on the phone had been very friendly. She had told her she would be waiting at the station, possibly with the children in tow, and not to worry about the cost of the journey, she would be reimbursed.

    Teresa fell asleep almost as soon as she boarded. When she woke, the train was climbing through forests and waterfalls. It had rained a lot over the previous weeks and water was gushing down the rock face. She couldn't see the sun, just slices of an intensely, uniformly blue sky. She tried to read, but after a few lines a swelling nausea made her close her eyes again. She was tired, she had been up since five o'clock, and she fell back asleep. The second time she woke was gentler. The train was running along a straight track. Through the window, Teresa saw the smooth surface of a vast, lead-grey lake. She looked at her watch. There was still an hour left. She picked up her book with slender hands (in such contrast to her strong and healthy body) but this time let herself be distracted by the verdant countryside rolling idly past on the other side of the lake. It was a beautiful day on this side of the Alps too; a wispy cloud floated across the sky. Teresa thought of her mother who had never left the village, and her older sister who probably never would either. And she laughed to herself with the naïve courage of youth. Outside the window, clusters of buildings began to break up the rural landscape. The train went in and out of stations and filled up with people speaking a language she couldn't understand. Thank goodness the parents are both Italian, she thought as she looked around, and that the children, for now at least, only used that language.

    Then the train pulled into the city, the end of the line. Teresa stepped down onto the platform with the patent leather handbag clasped to her chest and looked around. Everyone was hurrying towards the underpasses. She waited until she was almost the only

THE NEW JOB AND THE OWL

person left and then saw a woman running up the last few steps pulling a stroppy little boy behind her. She heard her speaking Italian as she yanked at his arm and thought it must be her. She smiled.

The woman was curt but friendly. She was wearing trousers and a crookedly fastened jacket. She didn't have any make-up on, and her hair was tied at her neck in a straggly bun.

'Ah, at last, here you are,' she said, as if it wasn't she who was late but the girl, and instead of shaking her hand, grabbed her arm while her other hand reached back to drag her hiding son out from behind her.

'Pietro, please! This is Teresa.' Introductions seemed unlikely. The woman looked at the girl, slightly narrowed her eyes and made an apologetic gesture with her head. They headed down a little side-street just outside the station where the woman had, rather poorly, parked her car. Little Pietro's thick chestnut-coloured hair fell into his eyes. He had thin shoulders and a scrawny chest and kept whining and dragging his feet along the tarmac. The woman marched resolutely ahead, bombarding Teresa with questions without listening to her answers, or so it seemed. In the car, she lit a cigarette and drove home with the windows down. The air was warm and spring-like.

The family lived in an apartment on the third floor of a tall building in an elegant street in the middle of town, not far from the cathedral. In the property, which felt very grand, there was an old lift which clanked upwards. As they slowly ascended, Teresa observed the woman: her thick hair streaked with grey, her beautiful, veiled almond-shaped eyes. There were deep wrinkles on the sides of her mouth and her birdlike face seemed somehow shadowed with pain. They entered the apartment. It was very big and light, with books piled up on the floor of the living room and so little furniture that Teresa asked the woman whether they had just moved or were just about to.

'No. We like it like this. Just the essentials. Everyone should live like this.'

Teresa didn't understand what this meant, and couldn't decide — at that moment or throughout her time in the house — whether or not she also liked that way of living. Next to the large French windows in an empty corner of the living room, the youngest child was playing with building blocks.

He lifted his head as they approached. 'Ciao, Giovanni,' his mother said. 'Where's Papà?'

'In there,' the child said, pointing with his chin towards the closed door.

'My husband's practice is through there,' the woman said, turning again to Teresa. 'You absolutely must knock first and then wait for an answer before entering. Even the children know that.'

Pietro detached himself from his mother and went to join his brother. There was only a year between them and, since the youngest was more solidly built, they looked as if they could have been twins. The woman took off her jacket and asked Teresa if she had eaten.

'On Sundays, we take *brunch*, you see,' she said, using the English word. 'A sort of breakfast-lunch at around eleven o'clock, so no one's ever hungry at this time of day. I can offer you some bread and ham and a slice of cake that a friend brought over yesterday.' She directed Teresa towards a kitchen chair and started to arrange the food on the table.

'I'll make some coffee,' the woman said in a louder voice, and soon her husband appeared in the kitchen doorway. Teresa noticed that the woman looked at him with a hint of disapproval.

'Ah, there you are. My husband,' she said, turning towards Teresa, who had stood up to hold out her hand.

The man shook it limply. Teresa looked at him. He was maybe a couple of years older than his wife, with pale, watery eyes behind thick-rimmed glasses. His face was unshaven around his plump lips. The younger son looked a lot like him, whereas the elder had his mother's sharp features and the same almond-shaped eyes. The man was wearing a flannel shirt buttoned up at the front, out of which sprouted skinny, hairless legs. The girl thought that he must have been about the same age as her own father, who she had never before seen in such a state of undress.

There was a moment of apprehension after they had said hello, but then the man asked Teresa, 'So, when do you start?' He was about to sit down but his wife burst out, 'Please!' before continuing in a more normal tone. 'Please, go and get dressed.'

'Sorry,' she said, turning towards the girl. 'We work so hard all week, on Sundays we let our hair down a bit...'

Teresa didn't understand — at home they got up early on Sundays and dressed their best for the ten o'clock mass — but she said 'of course!' and 'not at all!' in response. The man threw his wife a look that, to Teresa, seemed angry. Then he left. He came back half an hour later, dressed very smartly, but only to say goodbye and announce that he was going out. He had to see a colleague about a work thing.

※

Teresa's dark eyes now shone brighter against her slightly reddened face. She sat at the table, legs crossed, arms folded across her chest to hide where the button of her blouse was straining over her bust. It was like she had become twisted around herself in the grip of unfamiliar feelings of exhilaration and timidity. Exhilaration held back by timidity. Contradictory sensations stirred within her: the house was so bare, with no trinkets, not a single ornament, and there was something reckless about the children's parents, something not very grown up, as if they belonged to a generation midway between her own and her parents'. Back in her village, when people got married they became adults, or so it had always seemed to her, and however young they were they immediately lost any lightheartedness they might have possessed. She liked the children straight away, even if at first she feared they might not take to her.

To distract herself from her discomfort, Teresa began to eat the cake, breaking tiny pieces off with her fingers. The woman asked if she would like some milk and she answered, 'Yes, please.' The woman retrieved the milk from the fridge, got a glass and sat down opposite her. At that point, the children surrounded their mother, clambering up into her arms, still wary but also a little curious. Sometimes looking her in the eye, sometimes hiding their faces in their mother's hair, they started to inspect Teresa. Their mother, meanwhile, ran through their daily routine and explained what Teresa's tasks would be.

Suddenly, having crawled under the table, the children appeared at Teresa's feet, and she reached her hand out towards them. Giovanni stood up next to her and asked for some milk 'like Teresa'. His mother took a glass and Teresa poured some milk into it for the little boy. Teatime went on like this for another half hour. Before they went out again, the mother showed Teresa the 'nanny's room', right next to the children's bedroom: it was light, spacious, and in it there was a bed, a desk, a wardrobe and a bathroom all to herself.

Then, the mother, the children and Teresa went to the park together. When they accompanied Teresa to catch her train at about five, the children didn't want to let her go.

Sitting in her train compartment, Teresa felt happy, an exuberant feeling, bigger than the joy she had sometimes experienced at home. Now, finally, she had a space for herself; for the first time she had made a proper move out of the house and the village. She had a job in a well-to-do family who seemed determined to employ her without a fuss (they would take care of all the necessary documents). The work itself didn't worry her, and any strangeness she had noticed that day felt like an intriguing challenge. What's more, the children's mother had suggested that she enrol in a German course in the mornings while the children were at nursery.

When she got home she didn't say much about the interview. Just a few comments about the house and the scarcity of furniture and the many books she had seen piled up on the floor. To her father's slightly concerned questions, she just answered that, 'yes, the lady seemed a good person and the children very sweet.'

THE NEW JOB AND THE OWL

She said nothing more and a month and a half later, when all the documents were ready, she left with a large suitcase for her new job. She wouldn't be back until Christmas, and so she needed to pack summer and winter clothes. It could get rather chilly, even as early as September, the children's mother had told her.

※

In her first few months of work, Teresa had a lot to do. Settling the youngest boy into the Italian Krippe his brother already attended was quite quick, all things considered, but initially it meant she couldn't go to her German class. It was a private nursery with few children and it closed at four in the afternoon. Once a week, Teresa had to go and help in the kitchen, something she did very gladly, so much so that she sometimes offered to do this task in place of other mothers and babysitters. Pietro was considered something of a problem child because it was difficult to get him to play with the others, but he had become decidedly more sociable since his younger brother arrived (or maybe it was Teresa's presence which had improved things?). Giovanni lashed out often, but was very outgoing and won everybody's affections from the very first day. When the weather was good, after nursery they would all go to the park or walk along the river, but often it rained or a thick fog would gather, so they couldn't stay outside for long. Teresa would bring Giovanni and Pietro back home along with some playmates and their mothers or babysitters. She would make everyone a snack and keep an eye on the children's games.

At half past six when everyone went home, Pietro and Giovanni would have a bath, get into their pyjamas and at about seven have dinner with Teresa. The mother would bustle in breathlessly just before eight and often had no energy to play with the children. She would sit on the carpet with them for a while, distractedly build a tower, maybe exchange a few words with her husband and then she'd say, 'Can you sort them out please, Teresa?' She was almost nicer to her than to her own children. Sometimes they would do the school run together and then, before the girl dashed off to her German lesson, they would have a coffee and a gipfel in a cake shop just below the Krippe. In those moments, the mother was more relaxed and would recommend Teresa books or outfits, or tell her about films she had seen long ago. The father, in his white shirt, would only turn up to say hello at teatime. On occasion, he would come home between appointments to joke around with the children and from around eight o'clock he'd be back for good. His appointments actually finished at seven — that was when his assistant left, a sour, crabby, German-speaking woman of a certain age, who the children didn't like.

Sometimes the father would suggest that Pietro and Giovanni go into his office and do some drawing so that Teresa could tidy the kitchen and set the table for him and his wife, but the children almost always preferred to stay with Teresa. The only time they went along with it, back in the early days, they came back looking glum and Teresa thought they must have got bored in there with their father. The next time he called them through it was Teresa who said, 'Don't worry, they're no bother, they can stay here.' When they had finished playing of an evening, Pietro and Giovanni would put their building blocks away into a box with Teresa and wheel it into their room. Then they would go and see their parents, who would normally be in the middle of dinner, to kiss them goodnight. After that, Teresa would tuck them in and tell them a bedtime story.

Sunday was Teresa's day off. Sometimes the children's mother suggested she go see a film, and gave her money for the ticket and a little more on top. It was good language practice and Teresa gladly took advantage of it. And so, on Sundays in autumn she would arrange to meet Betta, one of the babysitters she had met at the Krippe, by the cathedral and together they would go to the cinema and then to the cake shop for a cup of tea. One Monday in October when the family had gone down to see relatives in Italy for the weekend, Betta, who was a few years older than her and had lived in the city for longer, took Teresa to a second-hand clothes shop and gave her a head-to-toe makeover. Teresa observed herself in the mirror, happy to look less and less like the girl who had left her village a few months before. These days, she wore her hair loose or casually tied back and, like her friend, hardly wore any make-up and dressed all in black. In the evenings, she read. When she finished the book her cousin had given her, a strange Russian novel, a sort of detective story, she read others. There were lots of books in the house and the children's mother constantly made recommendations. On Sunday evenings before settling down to read, Teresa would sit at the desk in her room and write short, reassuring letters to her parents and siblings.

Meanwhile, it had turned very cold. The days were getting shorter and more and more often after Krippe Teresa would come straight home with the children. One day at the end of October, Giovanni had a fever and so Teresa had to insist that Pietro go through to his father's office while she prepared a compress for the little one. When he came back with his father, Pietro was pale and his eyes wet and for the first time he refused to let Teresa put him to bed. His mum had just got back and she dealt with him. The next morning, the mother said he had been restless all night and that maybe it was best to keep him at home in case he was coming down with something too. Pietro cried when his mother left for work but then played all morning on his own in a corner. Teresa went back and forth between him and Giovanni. Every now and then, she put a cool hand to his forehead to check if he was hot. His temperature was in fact rising; Pietro too came down with a nasty bout of flu.

In those days when the children were sick, Teresa hardly left the house. She no longer had any time for reading or learning German. In the evenings when the parents got home, she would go out for long walks around the empty city. Sometimes Betta would accompany her for a while.

The little ones got exasperated with the long, dreary days and Teresa ran out of ideas to entertain them. She ended up calling home to ask her mother, who was originally from South Italy, the exact recipe for pizza dough. The pizza didn't turn out fantastically, but the children were very happy to spend an entire morning with their hands covered in flour and asked to do it again. In those days, she rarely saw either of the parents. She was tired and everything had begun to grate on her nerves: the whining children, the bare house, the grey city and the parents always being busy elsewhere. It was the first time she had missed home, her mother even, and her simple, comforting presence. But that didn't last long.

Finally the flu ended and to celebrate their recovery one Saturday the mother, father and children took Teresa to the ice rink. The children wanted to rent skates for her so that she could skate too. The mother taught her how to move her feet on the ice, holding the railing. The father read the papers and smoked outside on the wooden steps. He didn't know how to skate, the children said.

November drew to a close. The weather turned bitterly cold and the days were short. The children in town tottered through the streets all bundled up. Pietro and Giovanni had been back at the Krippe for a few weeks when one morning one of the two teachers on shift asked Teresa to follow her into a room that they used as an office. Sitting behind the desk was a woman with short grey hair who was introduced to her as the 'psychologist'. Assunta, the teacher, a second-generation Italian, was worried about Pietro because since he had come back after the flu he had started cutting himself off and playing on his own again. She asked if there was something going on at home, if Teresa had noticed anything out of the ordinary. Teresa tried to reassure the two women: it was probably just a bit of jealousy of his little brother, as now, even at the Krippe, Giovanni had marked his turf. His younger brother could be a little overbearing, and Pietro suffered from it sometimes... The psychologist interrupted her in stilted Italian and explained that his teachers had raised concerns once before, about a year ago. They suspected some form of mistreatment but they couldn't do anything about it unless someone reported it. They told her to keep an eye

THE NEW JOB AND THE OWL

out. Teresa's face became red and she mumbled, 'No, no, that's not possible, you must have made a mistake...'

✻

It was December, an array of lights shimmered all around, little festive markets popped up in the squares of the Old Town, under the porticos and in the entrance hall of the station. On Saint Nicholas Day, the children's parents brought home a real Christmas tree held up by a wooden stand and put it in the living room, decorating it with glass baubles they had brought down from the attic. The tree was a little bare but its resin released an intense aroma. It contrasted starkly with the huge artificial tree they had at Teresa's house, laden with flashing lights, tinsel and bows bought year after year from the small supermarket in the village. The children were lively and happy, their parents ate dinner with them and Teresa more often in those weeks of Advent. Their mother put the children to bed and sometimes mother and father went to the cinema to catch the last film. One morning just before the start of the holidays, the children's mother even wanted to take Teresa shopping. She took her to the centre of town where she bought her a warm jumper and some chocolates to take home to her parents and siblings. Teresa took this as confirmation that there was no truth in the hypothesis put forward by the teachers and psychologist that morning a few weeks earlier.

Then the Christmas holidays came around. The family was to go up to the mountains and Teresa back to her village for a couple of weeks. She was surprised by the immense joy she felt on seeing her father, mother and siblings, especially the little ones. She realised that she had missed that little house bustling with people, the huge artificial Christmas tree with all its trinkets and ornaments, and she threw herself wholeheartedly into the Christmas preparations with everyone else. Every so often, she would ask her mother about a certain recipe and take notes. Her stories were mostly about the Krippe. She spoke little of the family. Pietro's jealousy of his little brother, the absent parents... All things her parents wouldn't be able to understand, Teresa thought. By the end of the festivities, though, she was happy to leave again, to see 'her' children, to return to the city where she no longer felt quite so foreign.

※

January was a difficult month. The holiday didn't appear to have cheered the family up a great deal: the parents went back to being around very little during the day and Teresa often heard them arguing at night. The teachers at the Krippe complained. The children were restless and volatile, even when they were alone with Teresa. Pietro didn't want to go to nursery and had started wetting the bed again. She didn't know what to do.

One evening in late January, just after seven o'clock when Teresa and the children were eating, their father came into the kitchen and asked if they wanted to go into his office after dinner to draw. With a slow movement of his stubby, pasty fingers, he stroked the top of Pietro's head. The boy jerked around suddenly, knocking his bowl of tomato pasta, his favourite, onto the floor. Pietro began to sob and his father picked him up. 'Come on, let's go into the other room. When Teresa's finished cleaning up, we'll come back and get you another bowl of pasta. There's plenty left, do you see?' As he spoke, holding the boy in his arms, he leaned over the almost full pot.

Teresa tried saying that Pietro really was no bother, that he could stay there with her, but the father was already halfway across the room. She picked up the pieces of the bowl, threw them into the bin and cleaned the floor while Giovanni continued to eat slowly. Then she warmed up a small portion of pasta and put it onto a plate for Pietro. She called out to him but no answer came from the office. So she went into the living room and, without knocking, her heart in her mouth, opened the door.

Inside she saw the father with his unbuttoned white shirt and stethoscope hanging from his neck, sitting at the desk looking intently through some prescriptions. Little Pietro turned towards her,

THE NEW JOB AND THE OWL

he was standing on a stool by the window. It was snowing outside.

Teresa was overcome by shame and relief. Since she had been called to the Krippe a few months before, she had lost her sense of ease with both the children and the parents. In every gesture, even the most gentle and everyday, she saw something devious, alarming. Or was there *actually* something alarming? She wasn't even sure what she was looking for. She had no proof, and she felt guilty for betraying the people who had entrusted her with their children.

Eventually she decided she would speak to the mother. She told the teachers at the Krippe and they had supported her. They even said they would help her if she was dismissed from the house.

'No, they won't do that,' Teresa had responded calmly. 'The lady is a good person. She's not around much, but she loves her children. I'm sure that if what you said is true, she doesn't know anything about it, she hasn't realised, poor lady.'

And so one evening after putting the children to bed, Teresa joined the woman in the living room. Her husband was out and she was reading. She waited patiently until the woman looked up and then said, 'Ma'am, Ma'am, the children… they're not well. Pietro is wetting the bed almost every night…'

'Teresa, I've told you before,' the mother said impatiently, lifting her eyes from her book, 'Pietro is jealous, Giovanni is such an assertive child. I'll try to be around more in the next few months…'

'Ma'am,' Teresa started again, her eyes lowered, 'at the Krippe they said… the psychologist said… something about… abuse… But I don't believe it, Ma'am,' the girl hurried to add. Her face had turned a bright red, her hair was dishevelled, and she began to shake.

'Oh,' said the mother, suddenly hostile, 'they said that did they? Why the hell are they meddling in other people's business, and what right do they have talking to you about something like that? My husband is a good man, he has his faults, like all men for that matter, but he loves his children. And "abuse," what an ugly word!'

The mother stopped and stared at Teresa. She looked like a different person. Her skin was ashen, her beautiful eyes narrowed into two slits and her mouth folded down at the corners, her wrinkles deepened. Teresa thought her face was about to break, shatter into tiny pieces. But the mother continued, 'And what evidence do they have? Can you tell me what evidence they have, Teresa?'

'But Ma'am, they're your children, they're not well, if there's something not right, talk to the psychologist at the Krippe, they, they said they could help you...'

'Help me? Oh, sure! Don't you see — they're fixated on destroying my family! And now you're in on it too. Teresa, I expected more from you...'

'Ma'am, I just wanted to help,' said Teresa in a tiny voice. 'I love the children, I like your house, you've been so kind to me...'

'Oh yes,' the mother interrupted sarcastically, 'you want to help me? Then go and tell those bitches that everything is great here, that we can look after our own children just fine, thank you very much, and that every family has their difficulties and they have no right to poke their noses into other people's private lives. Things are complicated, Teresa. Life is never just black and white. You've risked dragging us all down, including the children, without even knowing what the problem is.' The mother seemed to be on the verge of tears but managed to hold them back.

She paused and then said, 'Now go, Teresa. Go to your room. Actually, no, wait, you'd better find yourself a new job in the next couple of months. I've been thinking of hiring a German-speaking girl for the boys anyway, perhaps someone from around here, they've got to start preparing for school and I'm looking for a German preschool for next year, one that's properly full-time, not one of these ridiculous co-managed places with their stupid lunches cooked by parents. What are they thinking? That we've got time to *burn*?'

Teresa looked at her and said nothing more.

'[…] My twenty years threaten me, Esterina, with their fatal green'

AMELIA ROSSELLI
La libellula (The Dragonfly)

'But for now, the stone is hungry and doesn't know how to say so.'

ANGELO MARIA RIPELLINO

18 NOVEMBER 2000
Belgium issues a stamp designed by Bob Buytaert for part II of the series The Twentieth Century in Eighty Stamps.

THE OWL

AS HER DAUGHTER LEAVES THE HOUSE AND closes the door behind her, the old woman's dream lingers behind her eyelids. As if expecting a guest, she tidies the pleats of her skirt on her knees, pats her almost white perm into place with both hands and lets out a long sigh. Sitting on the sofa next to the French doors that open onto the balcony, she pulls back the organza curtain and looks out into the early November evening. The bare trees cast long shadows and street lamps illuminate the grey lake. In her lap lie the beginnings of a knitting project, and next to her a ball of baby-blue wool alongside a crumpled book. Familiar sounds float in from the kitchen: running water, clattering plates, chairs being pulled in and out. Maria is doing the dishes and soon will join her in the living room. She will sit down opposite, her own knitting in her broad, placid lap, and look at her with grey, compassionate eyes. The old woman wonders when she will see her daughter again. She misses her already, even though Ester's unending judgement unsettles and confuses her. Sometimes she feels so shy in her presence that she can hardly speak.

Once again, the old woman rummages through her memories in search of reasons for the thick tension that chokes the space between her and her only daughter. Has it always been there? Is it because of what happened? In the first years of her life, Ester doted on her mother. Her father was not home much. He was a young engineer at the time, managing public works for their local town council. He was also responsible for taking provisions to a refugee camp out in the countryside, not far from where they lived. Not even that small town in a rich and neutral country was spared the precarity of the last years of the war. But people back then helped each other out, and it was not uncommon for Ester's father to bring someone home to share dinner with his little family, sometimes even to stay the night. Her mother, although uneasy being forced to keep such varied company, spent her days stockpiling flour, eggs, milk, sugar and sometimes a chicken to fill the stomachs of her husband, daughter and any guests that might arrive. As a little girl she was frail (because she was born two months early, she would explain to everyone). She ate little and vomited often. The doctor said she was suffering from an acute form of ketosis, a sugar deficiency typical in premature babies that, in her case, manifested in a sort of hyperactivity. Ester never sat still and would immediately devour any grain of sugar — scarce in those years of rationing — that she could get her hands on.

Since her father's death her mother has lived alone and Ester goes to see her once a week for Sunday lunch. And so on Sundays Maria, a woman of few words from Valtellina who has been helping in the house for more than thirty years, spends the day with her grandchildren. That Tuesday in November, Ester was forced to leave work in a rush as Maria had found the old woman in a hazy, disoriented state having slipped while getting out of bed. Alarmed, she called the doctor and then the daughter.

Ester, who lives in a city not far away, does not get to her mother's house until around eleven, just in time to bump into the doctor, an old school friend who, having finished the check-up, is reassuring the old woman: 'No, no need for hospital. A moment of confusion at your age is normal.' Then, smiling, he turns to Ester who is standing in the doorway with Maria, and says, 'She's already up and about.' As Ester walks him to the lift, he adds, 'Of course, if you could stay the night every so often...'

'No chance,' she replies curtly. 'You know how it is between us. I'd rather put her in a home if it comes to that.'

The lift door slides open and the doctor, a big, cheerful man with some awkward mannerisms, puts his hand on Ester's bony shoulder, which is still covered by her coat. With his eyes narrowed, he says, 'Don't worry. Maria will stay tonight, I've already asked her, and I can try to drop in regularly too.'

'Thank you, Pietro,' Ester concludes. Her eyes suddenly soften and she covers her friend's hand with her own. 'I have to save myself, you see, from maternal affection.'

When the war ended, with his savings and some help from his well-to-do in-laws, the engineer bought a house with a garden. The family made a home upstairs and he set up his office downstairs to save on time and transport. He asked his wife to take care of all the paperwork. They would have liked to have more children straight away; he especially wanted a son to one day take over his business but, having known poverty as a child, he constantly feared that there wouldn't be enough money or that they would lose it all suddenly. With his mind set on financial stability, the engineer continued to work for the council, but he also took on some private jobs on the side and gradually his business grew. Their financial circumstances improved, but he was never at home. It was invariably already late at night when Ester, tucked up in bed with the light out, would hear the keys in the lock and her father's steps along the corridor. He would push open her half-closed bedroom door, come in and bend over her, his coat emanating cold and the smell of many cigarettes. 'Is she asleep?' he would whisper to her mother who would stand in the doorway. The little girl would feign deep, regular breaths and her father would stroke her arm or head. 'She's asleep,' he would announce, before turning away disappointed.

※

Mother and daughter increasingly found themselves eating alone in silence, one opposite the other, with bowls of thick semolina porridge in front of them and the radio playing. Afterwards, as she washed the dishes with her back to her daughter, the mother would sing soppy love songs and tell the little girl complicated stories of betrayal and star-crossed lovers that she had read about or seen on-stage as a child. Ester did not enjoy those stories — as the old woman would later learn — so she would lay her head on the table in the crook of her elbow and pretend to be asleep. Once the dishes were done, the mother would go over to her and stroke her curls that were strewn over the table. When Ester stirred, she would send her to bed without even telling her to brush her teeth. Other times, the little girl would feel sick after dinner and so mother and daughter would run to the bathroom, brought together for several hours of that distressing ritual. Her eating issues had not stopped when the war ended, and her mother often wondered whether they were just dramatics rather than an actual illness. Even the doctor didn't believe her. He said that ketosis normally cleared up at around eight years old and that Ester was a tremendous fake. But despite the daughter's irritability and the mother's ways, despite the long silences of their lonely evenings, those years were a time of camaraderie for them both, and not only because of the spectre of that grotesque 'ketosis.' On winter afternoons, Ester gambolled about the house on her spindly legs as her mother buffed up the rubber plant's leaves with a cloth, sat darning socks in the living room or ironed in the dinette. The girl would stretch a length of knicker elastic between two chairs and practise the French skipping routine she had learned on the playground, or straddle an armchair holding a notebook and beg her mother to dictate the next day's homework. 'Just this once, Mammina!' and her mother would feel important because, even though she hadn't had much schooling, she had read a lot of novels as a girl and loved to make up stories.

The old woman sits on the edge of the bed with one foot in a slipper and the other still dangling mid-air. As if conjured, Ester reappears in the doorway without her coat, wearing a short grey dress that hugs her hips. She approaches on clicking heels and puts a hand on her mother's shoulder. At times, it seems as though the years will leave no trace on her daughter's body, the old woman thinks. Not her hands though, those strong, knotty hands with their coffee-coloured stains are not young hands.

'So, how are you?' Ester asks her, bending down to slide her mother's foot into the other slipper.

Like I've been shipwrecked and am holding onto a tree trunk for dear life, the mother wants to say. But she brushes it aside. 'You shouldn't have gone to the trouble of coming over, it's Tuesday, you're at work! And anyway, Maria's here.'

'What are you talking about?' Ester snaps. 'You had a fall, I was worried, I left halfway through a meeting...'

The old woman clenches up inside her fleece.

Ester should have had a brother, the old woman thinks now, or a sister. She and her husband knew it, they talked about it often. But after several years of hesitation, when they finally decided they were ready, the mother had three miscarriages in a row. At her first abnormal bleed, the doctor ordered bed rest, and Ester, who also wanted a little brother, went out every afternoon through the winter to get the shopping, laid the table for dinner and dried the dishes. A girl not much older than Ester, who already came twice a week to help out with housework, cooked their meals. After the first two miscarriages, Ester was sent with a little suitcase to Luciana, their

THE NEW JOB AND THE OWL

neighbour who lived with her four children and carpenter husband in a small house across the street. The third time Ester was told that her mother had lost the baby she was twelve years old and declared she would never go home. Her father went to collect her one evening in November — the old woman remembered this well — and somehow managed to convince her to return. From then on, discomfort wormed its way between the mother and daughter. Ester no longer followed her mother around the house, gambolling about on spindly legs on winter afternoons, but went to do her homework across the road at the neighbours' instead. She chose as her shelter the chaotic house where Signora Luciana repaired clothes to top up the household income and was always standing at the stove (the old woman knew this because the neighbours' kitchen window was directly opposite her bedroom window). The two oldest daughters were already schoolmistresses and in the afternoons they would help the children with their homework on the big walnut table while the ragù simmered on the stove and their mother bustled about in her greasy apron. Even Ester's food troubles cleared up in those months. How will she cope, my delicate little girl, the mother thought as, full of shame, she pulled back the white blinds of her bedroom window in the dimness of the afternoon to peer at what was going on across the street. But however many things she would have liked to ask her, when Ester came home and stood in front of her, all she could say was, 'How did it go? Did you finish your homework?'

 Ester would come back home as late as possible and shut herself in her room as soon as she had finished dinner. In the inevitable solitude of the afternoons, when she didn't have her husband's business accounts to work on, the mother took up knitting again and sat reading on the sofa. Sometimes, to return Signora Luciana's favour, she would bake her and her daughters an apple cake. She hoped that the familiar smell of the cake would revive her link to her daughter's heart, but when Ester got home from school she would pretend to not even notice it. With an impenetrable face, she would mutter hello and rush up to her bedroom.

In those years of rapid change and growth, it was not only homework that kept Ester away from home and her mother. From the beginning of high school, she would stay after school to play ball games with her classmates. Later, she started asking her father to take her with him onto construction sites and also attended dance and music lessons. Being one of her piano teacher's most talented students, she would often perform in the houses of notable people in the town. In a long, satin dress and with her face framed by thick, curly, copper-coloured hair held back by a white ribbon, she would barely look at the audience as she played. Her father, despite not being a great lover of classical music, would sit awkwardly on the austere settees. Although he was unable to relax in those sophisticated parlours, he was nevertheless proud of his bright, talented daughter who almost seemed to want to make up for not being a son. The old woman, on the other hand, entirely excluded by now from Ester's interests and endeavours, settled into a strained distance made up of attentive care, admiration and considerable sacrifice.

※

In the hope that our children will not resemble us, but be stronger and better than us. The words of a beloved writer give the old woman strength as she watches her daughter bend down and put her slipper onto her foot with a determined yank. 'Come on, let's head through,' she says. The old woman is weak, she leans on her daughter's arm and they move slowly down the corridor. Her slippers brush along the marble floor; her daughter is wearing heels. The two women do not speak. In the living room, the mother sits on the old sofa and a smile suddenly lights up her face.

'When I fell this morning, lying there on the floor, I thought that if I was going to die I'd have preferred it to be here, on the sofa.'

Ester senses that the old woman wants to hold her and stretches out her hand. 'It's going to be OK,' she says, trying to sound reassuring. 'It's normal at your age, Pietro said so.' Lifting up the ball of wool, she adds in a suddenly bright tone, 'You've started knitting again, well done!'

'A blanket for Maria's newest grandchild. He's due around Christmas,' the mother replies, quietly. A grimace passes over the daughter's face.

※

Ester's high school years were marked by a restrained exuberance. She excelled in everything: piano, dance, drawing, even ball sports, which she still played now and then with her old schoolmates. At school, she loved mathematics and art history but her grades were also brilliant in physics, literature and French. Her beauty lent her an air of sincerity, but the mother still sensed something hostile in her, something that could have morphed and thawed but instead, after what happened, ossified into a frame around her life. She was rarely home, but when she did come back to rest, she was kind and sometimes even sweet with her parents. Those were happy years for the old woman.

It was when her daughter was in upper school that Maria entered the household. She was resourceful and quick but also patient and everyone immediately took to her. She had been preceded by a line of inexperienced young girls who needed constant supervision, left dust in the corners of rooms and dish cloths dripping with water and detergent on the side of the sink. Maria was about ten years younger than the old woman, but her quiet confidence and simple affection made her seem wiser than her years. Her discretion won the trust of the married couple. She was a lifeline for them when, staring into the void left by their daughter who had gone to study in a city across the border, they found themselves hardly able to speak to one another. Maria was there when Ester, despite her father's disapproval, went abroad to study architecture. She was there when arguments between father and daughter turned sour. And she was there, too, when Ester fell pregnant in the middle of her degree.

Her parents were excited to welcome her back home and so did not know whether to be happy or sad when she announced that she would be getting married and continuing with her studies. The wedding, a modest ceremony in the registry office followed by a reception at the home of the bride, was the parents' first chance to meet Ester's partner, a reserved and polite art history student with dark eyes and olive skin. The old woman liked him a lot, but his mother, a severe teacher at a prestigious school, made no effort to hide her disapproval of her son's hasty decision. At the little reception, however, not even she was able to resist the contagious joy of Ester, who floated about the house with her dark curls falling down her back, perfectly at ease despite the visible bump already swelling beneath her loose linen dress.

It was September. Autumn brought balls of baby-blue wool (Ester didn't like pink) into the old woman's house and she knitted in the evening while waiting for her husband to come home. Ester, meanwhile, much to the delight of her admiring parents, was full of energy and sat exam after exam. Then, in the middle of a lecture one November morning, her waters broke. Helped by a classmate, she rushed to the hospital and as she was taken to the delivery room she happily gripped her husband's hand. The pregnancy had lasted its full term. The birth was drawn-out and strenuous for the young woman who, until the very last minute, stifled her screams. She let out a single final howl that was hoarse and sounded like it was coming from someone else's body. But the baby, a boy weighing four kilos, slipped out without a sound. A knot had formed in the umbilical cord, a rare and undetectable occurrence. He arrived into the world already dead.

The old woman hurried to her daughter in the hospital. The girl would not speak, she wouldn't even cry. She was propped up with pillows and stared stiffly into the blankness of the room. She hardly acknowledged her mother. The old woman went over to her bed, caressed her hair like she had done when she was little and then stood stock still next to the bed, her grey coat open and her handbag clutched to her chest. 'You're young,' she said after a while. 'You'll have other children.' At that Ester erupted in an excruciating wail. 'No more children, Mamma! Never again!'

✸

Her blossoming was abruptly and irreversibly suspended, the old woman thinks. The lively, capricious girl withdrew just on the cusp of womanhood. A necessary death, a necessary vehicle for our passions, the old woman thinks. Ester's every movement appeared to have stalled and her gaunt, stony face revealed only obstinance. Later, as a determined woman who put her work and career above all else, she rebuilt high walls around herself and patrolled them vigilantly. But not a flicker of the flame that still burned within her shone through when she was with her parents. Frightened by the hostility that seemed to sustain her, they no longer knew how to give comfort.

✸

The smell of sautéed vegetables wafts in from the kitchen.
'Mmmm, can you smell that, Maria's cooking risotto,' Ester says as she gets up from the sofa. She joins Maria in the kitchen. She helps her lay the table and, while setting the plates, asks gently after her children and young grandchildren. The radio is playing in the living room. The old woman knits with slow, mechanical movements. Her face is still pale, her thin lips have not regained their colour, but her blue eyes are bright, alert, as if chasing the end of the yarn.

✸

Ester's marriage did not survive the ordeal. A year later, the boy with the deep, dark eyes who the old woman had liked so much went to study in the United States on a scholarship and never came back. Ester threw herself into her studies and graduated on time. Her father suggested she go and work for him, just to start with, to learn the trade, but Ester firmly refused. She said she wanted to continue studying Piacentini and Libera, the architects on whom she had written her thesis. She was involved in a research project on 1930s Roman architecture and, for now, she wanted to stay at the university. Her father realised then that Ester would never work in the trade and grieved as though he had lost something forever.

    As his daughter pushed him away, he increasingly shut himself off. In those years, the early seventies, the construction industry was booming and there were building sites everywhere. By that point, the engineer was a known authority in the province. He set the standards and was wanted for all public works. During the day, he would run from site to site and every evening after dinner, he would go down to his studio to work. With his pencil in one hand and cigarette in the other, he would sketch designs and make calculations, and when the old woman, already in her nightie with a cardigan draped over her shoulders, went down to call him, he would immediately open all the windows to let the stagnant smell of smoke out, even if it was the middle of winter. 'Come on,' she would say and he, stubbing out his last cigarette in the ashtray, would shake his head and say, 'I don't get it, I just don't get it.' The old woman never knew if he was talking about his work or their daughter's distance.

※

When the risotto is ready, Maria calls the old woman for lunch. Ester looks annoyed as soon as her mother's thin figure appears in the kitchen doorway, her face still pale and frightened and the white curls of her perm a little ruffled on her forehead, shuffling her feet along the recently polished marble floor. 'Come on, don't act all sick! Eat this delicious risotto Maria has made and you'll feel better in no time, you'll see.'

    The old woman sits in her usual place opposite Ester, smiles nervously and asks her daughter again, 'Have you got to go back to work after this?'

'Of course, I told you already, I had to leave an important meeting to come here. We've moved it to five o'clock.'

Maria serves the risotto then sits down between mother and daughter. The old woman forces a smile and undoes the top buttons of her blue cardigan. Maria places her plump hand over the woman's small and bony one, squeezes it gently and says, 'Keep it on, Signora.'

'It's warm here in the kitchen,' says the old woman, looking at Maria. 'It's nice.' Then she lifts her gaze, 'Buon appetito.'

Her daughter has already started eating. See, the old woman thinks, how hard it is for her to be here, how she is disgusted by this everyday monotony and yet how she yearns for it. On the shelf just above Ester's head there is a photo of her, taken on the day of her graduation. Her serious face, her lovely wavy hair gathered at her neck, her dry gaze and a hint of bitterness on her lips.

※

The heart attack came all of a sudden one morning in June. Everything changed. While still in hospital, the father announced his plan to sell the house and find a smaller apartment for himself and his wife. 'You won't abandon us, will you, Maria?' he said to the maid who had come to the hospital to relieve the old woman. Perhaps he saw her as the fulcrum of his family, that was, at this point, without a future. Ester had dropped by on the first day, when her father was still in intensive care, on her way to Bochum to give a lecture that evening. It was a flying visit. She leaned over him after covering her elegant herringbone trouser suit with a green smock, stroked his hand and whispered to him, 'You have to make it, Papà, I can't stay, but you have to promise me you'll make it.' And at that moment the mother saw fear in her daughter's eyes.

The engineer underwent heart surgery and spent several months in hospital. He lost weight and was worn out by the forced inactivity; he started to see his isolation as neglect. Nobody truly needed him: not his wife, certainly not his daughter, not even his studio. He had employed an engineer around Ester's age ten years earlier when his daughter turned down the job, who by now was more than capable of taking the helm. In a dark mood of resignation, he moved from the rehabilitation unit back to the large apartment where he had hardly lived. With the ravenous eyes of a recent ex-smoker, his pipe cold between his teeth, he would wander around those big rooms as if in search of something to hold onto. He would lean on sofas and armchairs and rarely sit down. He was only ever truly happy when the young engineer or one of the designers came up to the apartment to ask for his advice on something. But unfortunately even this happened infrequently and he soon realised that those requests were not urgent or necessary in the slightest but rather the result of his colleagues' affection for him: he was no longer needed in the studio. Ester too, driven by fear, came more regularly after the heart attack. She was always in a rush and stayed for as little time as possible; there was always some article to submit or a lecture or class to finish preparing back home. At just over forty, Ester was already a professor and her articles were published in the top journals. Her father was very proud of her, but, while just a few months before he would obsessively try to bring up things they had in common, now architecture had all but vanished from their brief conversations. They talked about medicines, dietetic food, the weather. They didn't argue anymore. The old woman, who had never been able to mediate between father and daughter, now kept herself even further out of their way. For whatever reason, in her daughter's presence, she assumed responsibility for her husband's infirmity and whenever the two women found themselves alone, she would splutter confused excuses to which Ester would respond with her age-old, cavernous silence. In those days, the engineer found himself for the first time sharing daily life with his wife, something which was completely unknown to him. His health was not improving. In fact, he was getting weaker and looked increasingly absent as the weeks went by. His entire existence had suddenly taken on a slower, more cautious rhythm. Even the house, too big for that precarious new life, now seemed alien.

※

After they finish lunch, the old woman sits at the table for a while as Maria, with a stripy apron tied around her broad hips, clears away with gentle gestures and her daughter brews the coffee. The two women chat quietly. Maria, serene as ever, answers Ester's nervous questions. My daughter is so beautiful, the old woman muses as she flicks through the paper distractedly, with her sharp figure, her thick, silver-shot hair gathered in a bun and her slanting, elusive eyes. So beautiful and mysterious. She looks nothing like me, yet I feel more than ever that I belong to her.

※

The old woman moved alone into the new apartment with the view of the lake. The engineer meanwhile was living a separate life in a clinic not far from the house he had bought in which to live out his old age. White-haired and with dentures now useless in his sunken cheeks, his eyes, once blue, were now cloudy beneath round glasses with thick, black frames, similar to those of an architect he had greatly admired. He wandered along the white hallways muttering incomprehensibly. Sometimes his wife would find him like that, lost in the labyrinth of corridors, and the first thing he would say was, 'I'm looking for Ester, have you seen Ester?' His daughter visited him regularly but he would forget immediately afterwards, or perhaps he was just pretending not to remember.

Then, one cold morning in February, while Maria and the old woman were polishing the pewter tea set in the tidied apartment, the telephone rang. They were calling from the hospital. Somehow the engineer had managed to evade security and, dressed in only his cotton pyjamas, had slipped out just before dawn when the corridors of the clinic were already bustling with trolleys and nurses, and headed towards the garden. His unstable footing must have caused him to trip on the stone steps. He had rolled down to the foot of the sequoia tree where the road begins. They found his body some hours later.

※

When she finishes reading the paper in the kitchen, the old woman announces that she's going to go and have a lie down in her bedroom. Already standing, she turns to say goodbye to her daughter. 'See you Sunday,' she says, her eyes lowered, but Ester replies unexpectedly, 'I've changed my mind, I'll wait here until you wake up, let's see how you're feeling. And perhaps I'll come and stay over the next few days.' The old woman seems to see a light flicker in her eyes. 'I'll catch up on the meeting tomorrow.' She's scared, the old woman thinks, like when her father was in hospital. Perhaps our children need this, our vulnerability. They need to see that in our vulnerability we trust them.

Then, without turning on the light, the old woman goes into her room, falls onto the bed and sinks into the soft silence of the first afternoon of winter. She dreams of cycling through the woods. In the basket of her bicycle, among the dry and jagged leaves, a little owl looks out into the darkness with large, child-like eyes.

TRANSLATOR'S NOTE

'The New Job' and 'The Owl' are stories selected from Anna Ruchat's Swiss Literature Prize winning *Neptune's Years On Earth* (*Gli anni di Nettuno sulla terra)*, a collection of twelve short stories structured around the twelve months of the year. The stories are set over four decades from the 1960s to the early twentieth-century, and each is prefaced by an epigraph referencing a real-life event that took place in the same month and year – from the foundation of the Swiss Society for the Cultivation of Gardens in 1983 to bombings of the Gaza strip in 2008. While the epigraphs remind us of the macro-structure of historical events taking place at the time of each story, the stories themselves zoom in on characters' ordinary lives, floating lightly upon the ebbs and flows of human relationships and artfully delving into themes of family, time, loss and potentiality.

The stories that we have translated for this collection are the stories for June and November. Both stories narrate events in the lives of young women 'on the cusp of womanhood', but from rather different perspectives. 'The New Job' follows Teresa, a young au-pair living away from her parents for the first time and determined to forge a life bigger than theirs, while 'The Owl' is told from the perspective of an elderly woman reflecting on her strained relationship with her now-adult daughter. Both stories linger on the interrelatedness of our lives, the dynamic between the choices we make and the context they are made in, leaving the reader wondering about the balance between what-could-have-been versus what-inevitably-was.

'The choices we make and the context they are made in' feels an appropriate description of the process of co-translation too. Translating always involves a long period of fine-tooth-combing, tinkering with words, syntax and punctuation. But when there are two of you doing it, and every tiny difference in understanding or style usually comes down to your own individual cultural contexts (should her shirt be stretched 'tight' or 'taut?' Does organza curtain or net curtain feel more like what this woman would have had? Can you imagine skipping over knicker elastic? I'm not so sure…), you spend hours over tiny decisions that you'd likely have made intuitively on your own. But it also means you get a much deeper, more layered understanding of the text, and you get to explore all that richness with another passionate reader who is just as enthusiastic about discussing commas and knicker elastic as you are. And for a translator it doesn't get much better than that.

+SVIZRA is a series of eight chapbooks showcasing contemporary writing translated from the four official languages of Switzerland: German, French, Italian and Romansh. In giving equal visibility to each of the four languages, **+SVIZRA** offers a range of Swiss writing never before seen in English from a diverse group of some of the best authors living and working in Switzerland today, including National Literature Prize winning Anna Ruchat, Iraqi exile Usama Al-Shahmani and treasured Romansh author, Rut Plouda.

+SVIZRA is the result of Strangers Press' latest exciting collaboration with an international group of authors, translators, publishers, designers and editors, all made possible by generous funding from Pro Helvetia.

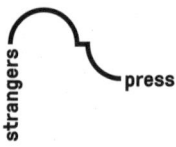

Supported By

University of East Anglia

NORWICH
UNIVERSITY
OF THE ARTS